JF
MADDOX

D0168684

JEFFERSON COUNTY LIBRARY
NORTHWEST BRANCH
5680 STATE RD. PP
HIGH RIDGE, MO 63049

NO LONGER PROPERTY OF
JEFFERSON COUNTY LIBRARY

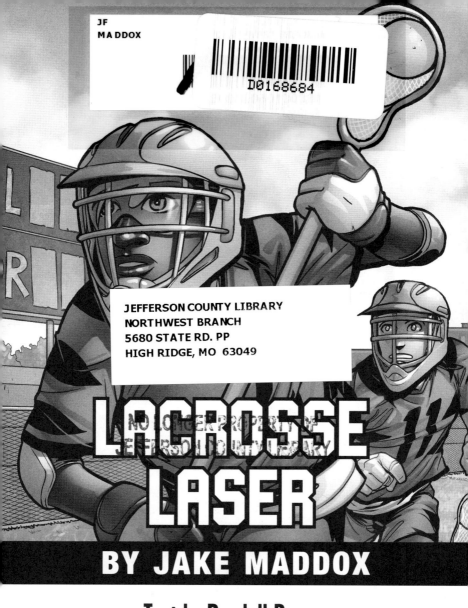

LACROSSE LASER

BY JAKE MADDOX

Text by Randall Bonser
Illustrated by Aburtov

STONE ARCH BOOKS
a capstone imprint

JEFFERSON COUNTY LIBRARY
NORTHWEST BRANCH

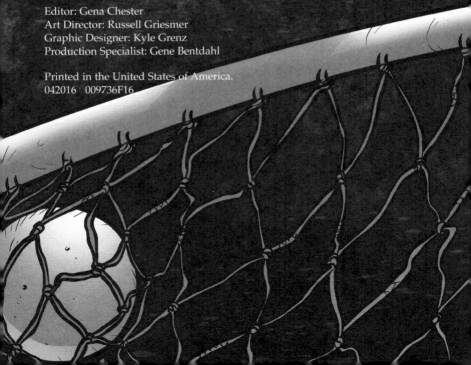

Jake Maddox Sports Stories are published by Stone Arch Books
A Capstone Imprint
1710 Roe Crest Drive
North Mankato, Minnesota 56003
www.mycapstone.com

Text and images © 2017 Stone Arch Books

All rights reserved. No part of this publication may be reproduced in whole or in part, or stored in a retrieval system, or transmitted in any form or by any means, electronic, mechanical, photocopying, recording, or otherwise, without written permission of the publisher.

Library of Congress Cataloging-in-Publication Data
Cataloging-in-Publication data is available on the Library of Congress website.

ISBN 978-1-4965-3051-6 (library binding)
ISBN 978-1-4965-3053-0 (pbk.)
ISBN 978-1-4965-3055-4 (eBook (pdf))

Summary: Jaylin has always been a good defender on the lacrosse field, but when he gets glasses, he has the chance to take his game to midfield. Does he have what it takes to help bring his team to victory?

Editor: Gena Chester
Art Director: Russell Griesmer
Graphic Designer: Kyle Grenz
Production Specialist: Gene Bentdahl

Printed in the United States of America.
042016   009736F16

TABLE OF CONTENTS

CHAPTER 1

THE DEFENSE HOLDS

Jaylin Buckley waited on the balls of his feet. As the Tigers' central defenseman, he had learned to watch his opponent's stick, not his eyes.

The Scorpions' attackman in front of him faked left, but Jaylin wasn't buying it. The guy's stick, a shorter version of Jaylin's long defensive stick, had stayed on his right shoulder. Clearly, he was not going left.

Suddenly, the attackman broke right and sprinted toward the Tigers' goal. If he got the ball in the net, he would tie the score at six. Jaylin moved quickly, matching his opponent step for step. As the attackman brought his stick back to shoot, Jaylin brought his up for a check. He lifted the guy's hands just enough to thwart the shot.

Seeing he had no shot, the attackman kept the ball and ran around behind the goal. DeAndre, Jaylin's best friend and fellow defenseman, followed him. Jaylin sprinted back to the center of the attack area, in front of the goalie, where an open attackman was calling for the ball.

The Scorpions passed the ball back up the attack area to Jaylin's right. He kept one eye on the Scorpion with the ball, and the other on the pesky attackman by the crease.

"30 seconds!" yelled Coach from the sidelines. If the Tigers could hold the Scorpions off for a half minute, they would keep their grip on first place in the league standings.

Suddenly, the guy with the ball faked out the defender in front of him and broke for the goal. As the ball carrier neared the crease, he faked a shot and zipped it to the attackman calling for the ball in the middle.

But Jaylin had seen it coming. A step behind the middle attackman, he lunged forward and got his stick on the ball just before it reached his opponent. The ball bounced right to Mateo, the Tiger's goalie, who scooped it up and let out a triumphant WOOP!

"Matty, we can still score!" Jaylin yelled at Mateo. With his head turned toward the goalie, Jaylin sprinted out of the attack area toward midfield. Mateo turned toward him and prepared to throw a long pass.

"No!" yelled Coach. "Find Dee! Find Dee!" Mateo turned and passed to DeAndre, who ran sideways until time ran out.

Tweet! Tweet! Tweet! Jaylin's team, the Tigers, were still in first place! Cheering, the boys ran to the sidelines. Jaylin walked slowly behind them. He was happy with the win, but Coach's instructions — not to pass it to him — bothered him. Nevertheless, he joined the circle of players forming around Coach.

"Great game today, boys," Coach said, laughing. "A little too close for comfort, though."

Jaylin tugged off his heavy gloves as Greg, an attackman, approached. "You shut that dude down in the middle, Jay!" he said.

"As usual, our defense was amazing," Coach went on. "And we had just enough offense to pull out a win. But, boys . . ." Coach frowned. "I don't think this level of offense is going to win in the playoffs. We'll need to find three or four more goals per game if we want to go any further. Where are we going to find some offense?"

No one said anything. DeAndre cleared his throat.

"Coach, maybe you could let Jay play attack some time? In practice he's got the hardest shot on the team."

"It's a laser!" Greg said. Everyone laughed.

Coach looked doubtful. "I'd love to play Jaylin on offense. I know he's got an amazing shot. And his footwork is as good as anyone in the league. But …"

"But I can't catch," Jaylin mumbled.

"I was going to say we need your awesome defense," Coach said.

"We can adjust on defense," DeAndre said. "We just need some more offense."

Coach scratched his head. "The truth is, Jay, your catching really does need to improve. To play attack, you have to be able to catch the ball consistently. For now we'll keep the lineup as it is."

Jaylin knew Coach was right. He hated the fact that he couldn't catch very well. No amount of practice seemed to help. He missed a lot of the passes thrown to him.

Jaylin had been put on defense, where his quick feet and aggressiveness were great for stopping opponents' attackmen ... and where he didn't have to catch many passes. The goalie usually started the Tigers' clears by passing out to DeAndre, who passed it to a midfielder, who ran forward to start the offense and find an open attackman. Jaylin really wanted to play midfield, where his speed would allow him to help with both attack and defense.

But Coach is right, Jaylin thought. *My catching just isn't good enough to play middie. And it probably never will be.*

CHAPTER 2

LEFT SIDE REVELATION

At practice on Tuesday, the team began by practicing cradling, turning the stick to keep the ball in the pocket. They practiced two-handed cradling, then one-handed cradling, which kept the ball secure while running. They also worked on stick checks, where a defensive player hits the stick of the person carrying the ball to dislodge it.

Then they practiced passing to each other. Jaylin paired up with DeAndre. As usual, he missed about half the passes.

"Maybe someday I'll get bit by a super spider, and suddenly I'll be the world's best catcher," Jaylin said, sighing. "'Cause this is not working."

"I wonder, Jay. . . ." his friend said.

"What?" Jaylin asked.

"Let's try an experiment," DeAndre said. He threw ten passes to Jaylin's right side. Jaylin caught nine out of ten. Then Dee threw the same number to Jaylin's left side. He caught one out of ten.

"Wow, I never noticed a pattern before," said Jaylin.

"This may be a dumb question, but when was the last time you had your eyes checked?"

Jaylin thought about it. "I guess it's been a couple years."

"You might want to get them checked again," DeAndre said.

After passing drills, the team worked on foot speed, staying in front of the ball handler, and defensive concepts. Then offensive concepts. Then they scrimmaged. Coach always let Jaylin play attack for a little while in scrimmages.

During the scrimmage, Jaylin sent one laser after another into the goal. Top left corner. Top right corner. Bottom left. Bottom right. Hard bounce over the goalie's stick.

"How do you do that?" asked Greg, the right attackman. "I'd be an all-star if my shots were that good."

"And I'd love to catch like you," Jaylin said.

"Let's combine skills," Greg said.

"I wish."

After practice, Coach gathered the players by the bench. "The good news is, we only need to win one of our two last games to make the playoffs."

"How 'bout we win both, and show everyone who's boss?" DeAndre said.

"Yeah!" everyone cheered.

JEFFERSON COUNTY LIBRARY
NORTHWEST BRANCH

CHAPTER 3

A NEW VIEW

"Which is clearer, one ... or two?" Dr. Keen asked as she turned the dials on the clunky machine in front of Jaylin's face.

"Two."

"Okay, which is clearer, two or three?" More clicks and little circles of light. Letters came into, went out of, focus.

"Three." This went on for ten minutes. Then Dr. Keen pulled the giant machine away from Jaylin's face.

"Your prescription has changed quite a bit in your left eye," said Dr. Keen. "We'll order a new prescription and you'll notice a difference immediately."

"Why has it changed so much?" Jaylin's mom asked with a worried look. "Is there something wrong with Jay's eye?"

"Mom, you worry too much," Jaylin shook his head.

"No," Dr. Keen explained. "It's common for a child's eyesight to change during growth spurts. The new lenses will help."

"Hopefully they'll help me catch better," Jaylin said.

"I can't promise that," Dr. Keen said, "but you'll certainly see the ball more clearly. It might take a little time for your brain and reflexes to catch up to each other."

They ordered new, stylish glasses in the optician's office.

"Mom, can I get athletic goggles too?"

"I'm not sure, honey. They're kind of expensive."

"But Mom, they'll fit better under my facemask," Jaylin said. Then he grinned slyly. "And my regular glasses won't get broken when I play."

"You've got a point," said Mom. "Okay, let's order some athletic goggles."

"Thanks, Mom!"

"But Jaylin," Mom said seriously. Jaylin looked at her. "If I'm going to spend this much money, I want you to really commit to improving your game."

Jaylin stood up. "I promise."

***

The goggles arrived on Friday. He and DeAndre tossed in Jaylin's yard.

"You look like you're about to fly one of those old fashioned airplanes with those goggles," Dee said.

"Hey, they're not supposed to be pretty. They're flatter against my face than my glasses. And they wrap around so I'll be able to see side-to-side a lot better."

"Cool. Then after the game you can go write a message in the sky with one of those little smoke airplanes."

"Let's just smoke the Bears tomorrow," Jaylin replied.

"You know it!"

They threw slowly at first, and close together. Gradually they began backing up and throwing harder passes.

"Hey, you're doing it!" Dee said.

"Doing what?"

"Catching passes on both sides!"

Jaylin smiled. "I guess I am." Just then DeAndre threw a pass high and to Jaylin's left. He swooped it out of the air nice and clean, then cradled it with one hand as he ran straight at his friend. "Jaylin Buckley breaks for the goal, with only one slow, lazy defender in his way!"

He faked to the left and executed a slick roll dodge to get around his friend. Dee flattened him with a hard check. Jaylin laughed and groaned as he lay on the grass.

DeAndre reached to help him up. "Too bad the new goggles haven't made you smarter!"

CHAPTER 4

A CHANCE AT MIDFIELD

The Tigers circled their coach just before taking the field against the Bears.

"These guys have a strong defense, but not such a great offense," Coach reminded them.

"Coach, can Jaylin play middie today?" DeAndre asked.

"Hmm," Coach said, rubbing his chin.

"He got his eyes fixed," DeAndre said. "Let's get him involved in the offense."

Coach chuckled. "Jaylin, you need to hire this guy as your agent. Sure, now that you have your new glasses, we'll try you out at midfield. I can't put you on attack, because I need you to help out with the defense."

Coach looked at DeAndre. "You ready to play center defense? You'll have to take charge of the D, Dee."

"I got this, Coach."

"Okay. Jay, you're taking the face-off. Might as well get you involved right at the start."

Jaylin crouched at midfield with the head of his stick next to the ball. His heart pounded and he felt the breath of the player crouched across from him. The whistle blew. Lightning fast, Jaylin covered the ball with his stick head and dragged it to the side. His opponent lost his balance and lifted his stick. Jaylin scooped up the ball and ran toward the Bears' net.

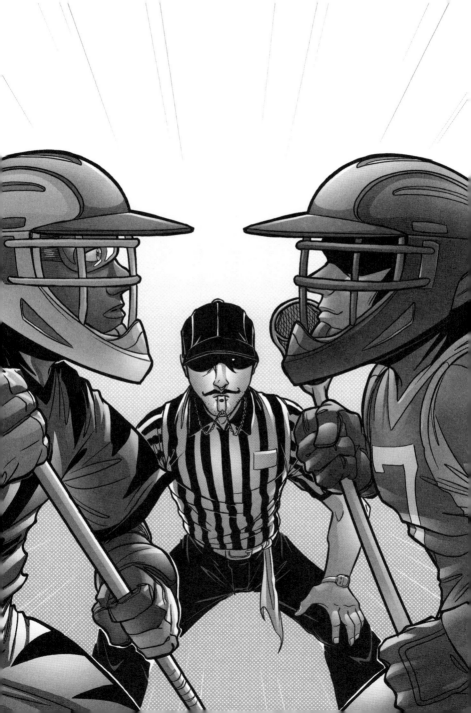

As he approached the attack area, he whipped the ball to Greg, who was closing in from his right. It felt great to run the whole field.

At first he hung back when his team was on offense, near the center of the field, so that he could dart back to help on defense. In the second quarter, Jaylin realized he was running the offense. Most of the passes ran through him at the top of the box before they went to either side or into the middle.

At halftime, the Tigers were leading 7 to 6.

"I think we've found our offense!" Coach could barely contain his smile.

"You're doing great," said DeAndre, pounding Jaylin on the back so hard he coughed out his mouthful of water.

In the third quarter, it was clear that the Bears had adjusted their game to the Tigers' new lineup. They put a floating midfielder near Jaylin the whole time, disrupting passes and blocking his progress with hard checks.

Jaylin felt like he was working twice as hard to accomplish half as much as he had in the first two quarters. Halfway through the quarter, the Bears tied the score at seven after a series of quick passes in the attack area.

"Jaylin, you have to play defense, too!" yelled Coach as Jaylin stood with his hands on his knees at midfield. After the face-off, the Bears broke toward the Tigers' attack area. A quick pass to the side, then a quick shot, which Mateo stopped.

Jaylin, still near the center of the field, held up his stick for the outlet pass.

Mateo turned toward Jaylin, then hesitated. Looked the other way. Looked back.

"Hit me!" Jaylin yelled.

"Do it!" DeAndre yelled.

"One minute!" Coach yelled.

Mateo reared back and launched a pass toward midfield. The ball went long, forcing Jaylin to run toward his left side. Fear gripped him. Why had Matty thrown the ball to his bad side? *Wait, I got this fixed. I can do this.* He reached out his stick to catch the pass.

And missed the ball completely.

A Bear midfielder scooped up the ball and broke for the Tigers' goal. An attackman sailed in from the right. As DeAndre popped up in front of the first attackman, the guy flipped a hard pass to his teammate, who was running in front of the goal completely alone.

Whiiish! The ball found the upper right corner of the net. Bears 8, Tigers 7.

The Bears exploded in cheers. The quarter wasn't over, but Jaylin felt like the air had been knocked out of his lungs. The rest of the team looked dazed too. Coach let another midfielder take the face-off, which he lost, and the ref soon blew the whistle. The Tigers walked off the field dejected.

"What's up?" Jaylin asked DeAndre. "Why was that guy all alone on the crease?"

"We're used to you running the defense," DeAndre said, panting. "You're faster than me. I can't keep up with their attackman."

"You've got to anticipate what he's going to do, Dee!"

"I'm not a mind reader like you," said DeAndre. "And besides, our middies aren't getting back to help."

"I'm tired!" Jaylin complained.

"Who's not?" demanded DeAndre. "And how could you miss that pass? Matty threw it right to you!"

"I don't know, it was to my left."

"You got that fixed!"

"Yeah, like a whole week ago!" Jaylin grabbed his water bottle. "Give me, like, a minute to get it right."

"How about ten minutes?" DeAndre demanded. "Otherwise we're out of first place!"

Jaylin and DeAndre were nose-to-nose. "It doesn't matter how many minutes we have if you guys can't stop their attack!" Jaylin was shouting now.

"Stop it, both of you!" Coach grabbed both boys by the shirt and pulled them back into the circle. "Up till now you've all played an amazing game. We fell apart there at the end of the third, but they're only up by one."

"I can't do it, Coach," said Jaylin with his head down.

"What do you mean?" asked Coach. "You can't do what?"

"I can't catch yet."

"That's not true! You caught . . . more than usual." Coach looked uncomfortable.

"I missed when it counted. I want to go back to defense."

Coach kicked the grass. "Okay, Jaylin, go back and take over the middle of the defense. DeAndre, back to left D. Damien, back to middie and face-off. Everyone okay?"

No one answered. "All right, get back out there and let's get one back."

They didn't get anything back. The Bears scored twice more, winning the game 10-7.

"I thought we had our offense figured out," Damien said.

"I know," said Coach. "I thought so too. But we broke down and I'm not sure what we're going to do next week. If the Bulldogs win today, which they should, that will put us in third place. We will have to beat them next week to make the playoffs."

"I hope I can help more than I did today," Jaylin muttered as he walked off the field. "Where's that super spider when you need it?"

CHAPTER 5

BACK TO DEFENSE

On Monday, Jaylin texted DeAndre.

"Sorry for what I said on Saturday. Practice at my house after school?"

Soon his phone buzzed.

"UR a jerk. See you there."

After school, the friends practiced their passing and catching. They passed standing still. They passed while running. They passed turning in circles. They even passed backward, tossing the ball over their shoulders while running one behind the other. Jaylin only got hit in the head once.

After a while, DeAndre said, "You have a harder time catching it while you're running. You're great when you're standing still."

"Great, we'll create a new play called The Statue of Liberty. I'll just stand in the middle of the field while you guys run around." Jaylin stood with one hand up like the famous statue.

"You're getting better. I think it might just take more practice. Lots more."

"Actually, the eye doctor said it might take a while before I saw any improvement. Okay, let's try the running drill again."

"Can't," said Dee. "Gotta get home and eat dinner. Mom just texted me."

"She is the mortal enemy of our team."

"No, that would be your left hand. If we can get that thing on our side, we're going to beat those Bulldogs."

"Yeah, but how?"

"With about a thousand more catches, that's how. See you tomorrow."

"Later," Jaylin said as the boys bumped fists.

***

At Tuesday's practice, Coach made Jaylin play defense for the entire scrimmage.

"I'm catching better with my left hand," Jaylin said as he took a water break.

"Yeah, I can see that," Coach said.

"Maybe I could play middie for a little bit in the game Saturday."

Coach was silent for a few seconds. "I need you to anchor our defense against the Bulldogs. Their offense is the best in the league."

"Okay," Jaylin said.

"I want you to work with Greg and show him how to improve his shot. He can work on it during the scrimmage. Maybe we can generate some more offense."

"Okay," Jaylin said. He fought to keep his disappointment from showing to the other guys. He'd had one chance to play midfield and he'd blown it. The only thing to do now was concentrate on defense.

"If we win this Saturday, it will all be worth it," Jaylin said to himself.

He almost believed it.

JEFFERSON COUNTY LIBRARY
NORTHWEST BRANCH

CHAPTER 6

FALLING BEHIND

Saturday morning was overcast and gray. A light rain soaked the field.

"This slick field gives them an advantage because they're not as fast as we are," said Coach. "It's going to slow us down. Here is the starting lineup."

Jaylin was playing center defenseman. Part of him was glad to be back at his old position, but another part wished he was back at midfield. Running the entire field and helping run the offense had felt natural to him.

"Let's do this," DeAndre said. "If we get to the playoffs we'll keep practicing so you can play middie."

"Is it that obvious?" Jaylin asked.

Dee laughed. "To me it is! But let's win this game first."

The Bulldogs won the face-off and set up their offense. Jaylin was surprised to see two attackmen run straight to the middle, by the crease, and wait for a pass. Most teams sent only one guy into the middle at first. The other Bulldog attackman and the three middies crisscrossed and ran cutting patterns, passing the ball back and forth to keep possession. They pressed forward with aggressive passes and cuts until—WHAP! A middie on the side slipped a beautiful shot past Mateo.

After the Bulldogs won another face-off, it was clear to Jaylin that they had scouted his team. They brought all six offensive players toward the goal without any concern about their defense. They scored again on their second trip down the field.

Jaylin yelled at his Tiger middies to move their feet on defense and stick with their man. They would have to help out against the Bulldogs' blistering attack. So far, they just seemed to be standing around, waiting to start the offense. But there would be very few scoring opportunities if their defense had to keep playing three-on-six.

After a furious ten minutes, the Bulldogs were up 4–1. The Tigers' one goal had come on a lucky long-range shot from Greg that had bounced on the ground over the Bulldog goalie's stick.

"They aren't even bothering to play defense," Jaylin said to DeAndre after the first quarter.

"They know they don't really have to," Dee said, taking a drink.

"Hey, you guys haven't been exactly a stone wall in the back either," said Coach, who didn't look too happy.

"They're bringing the whole team down into the attack area," complained DeAndre.

"Middies, you've got to come back and help on defense. They're killing us back there," Coach said. The whistle blew. "A little tighter on defense and a lot more aggressive on offense, all right?"

They brought their hands in. "One, two, three, TIGERS!"

The second quarter was a little slower. The Tigers midfielders tried to keep the ball from coming into the middle of the field. That gave the defense a little room to breathe and be aggressive in their man-to-man defense.

But with the Tigers' midfielders playing on their own half of the field, the team couldn't generate any offensive threat, either. Their few offensive possessions were broken up without much trouble by the three Bulldog defensemen. Just before halftime, Greg scored on another long shot to bring the Tigers to within two.

At the half, the score read Bulldogs 4, Tigers 2.

CHAPTER 7

STEPPING UP

"We need some offense, boys." Coach looked around the circle. "And we need it now. Otherwise we're watching from the sidelines next week."

The boys were silent.

"Let me play middie," Jaylin said suddenly. "We're already losing, so it can't get any worse. They're barely even playing defense. It's embarrassing. Let's make them pay for it."

"Yeah," several boys said.

Coach had a sparkle in his eye. "DeAndre, you ready to go back to center D?"

"Let's do it," Dee said. "Let Jay take the face-off and send everyone forward. Score a quick goal so they don't know what hit 'em."

"It could backfire if Jay doesn't win the face-off," Coach said.

"I'll win it," Jaylin said, with more confidence than he felt.

"Okay, Jaylin, you'll take the face-off. Damien, you'll move to left middie. DeAndre, center D. Boys, this better be the best half you ever played if you want to make the playoffs."

The face-off was a scramble. Jaylin pushed against the opposing face-off specialist as they clawed for the ball. Just as the Bulldog player was going to clamp the ball, Jaylin batted it to the side. Without pausing, he scooped it up and tore toward the Bulldogs' goal. It seemed to take everybody by surprise. The Tigers had six guys barreling toward the goal.

As Jaylin advanced toward the goal, he saw Zach, the Tigers' left attackman, with a sliver of space in front of him. Jaylin whipped the pass to where Zach was about to be. Zach caught it and used a nice roll dodge. As the Bulldogs converged on Zach, Greg charged in from the right with his stick in the air. Zach found it and lobbed a perfect pass to Greg.

A defenseman put a big hit on Greg, but was a fraction of a second too late. Greg's shot hit the top right corner of the goal.

The entire play had taken about ten seconds. The Bulldogs looked stunned, and now the Tigers had cut the deficit to 4–3.

Jaylin won the face-off again, this time by sweeping the ball behind him to DeAndre. Dee scooped it up and passed it quickly to Greg, who was streaking forward on the right.

Jaylin positioned himself in the center, at the top of the restraining line. This time the Bulldogs' defense was quicker, and stopped the immediate attack. The Tigers passed the ball around the back of the goal and back up to Jaylin. He passed it back to Zach on his left and it went around the goal again.

On the right side, Greg faked a pass back to Jaylin at the top. The defense tried to rotate, but not fast enough. With the ball still in his possession, Greg used a face dodge — bringing his stick up like he was going to shoot, then quickly crossing it to his weak side — to fool the defenseman in front of him.

With the defender off balance, Greg broke for the goal. Jaylin followed him. As the center defenseman checked Greg hard in the middle, Greg flipped the ball behind him. Jaylin took the pass on his right side and without pausing whipped it by Greg's head into the upper-corner of the goal.

Greg laughed. "Uh, that was a little close," he said as they walked back to midfield. "I could hear it blast by my ear."

"Your head made an awesome shield," Jaylin said. "The goalie never saw it coming."

Bulldogs 4, Tigers 4.

Jaylin lost the face-off and the Bulldogs started a slow, measured attack. Jaylin kept moving in the center of the field and reminded his fellow middies to keep moving, too.

"Stone wall in the middle," he said.

"Stone wall," they answered.

The ball came back to the middle. Jaylin intercepted it and charged up field. As he neared the Bulldogs' goal, he passed it to Greg on the right, who ran around behind the goal. Jaylin trotted right up to the crease, where Robert, the Tigers' center attackman, was standing.

"What are you doing?" asked Robert. "This is my spot."

"I know. Get ready," Jaylin said. He called for the ball, holding his stick up and running toward Damien, his fellow middie, who had the ball outside the attack area. Damien threw him the ball. Jaylin caught the pass on the right side of his head and whipped it straight back behind him without looking. Robert shouted in surprise, but caught the pass and shot. And missed.

As the quarter ended, the score remained Bulldogs 4, Tigers 4.

CHAPTER 8

PLAYOFFS OR OUT?

"Do you have one more quarter left in you?" Coach asked.

"Yeah!" shouted most of the Tigers. Jaylin kept quiet. So far, he had been able to keep everything on his right, but he wasn't sure how long he could keep that up.

"Play your best ten minutes and we'll be in the playoffs," Coach said as the team put their hands in.

"One, two, three, TIGERS!"

Jaylin clamped his stick over the ball during the face-off. He held it there until he felt the pressure from the Bulldog across from him let up just the littlest bit. He put his shoulder into the Bulldogs' attackman, shoved him off the ball while scooping it up, and ran toward the goal.

The Bulldogs had adjusted to the Tigers' new Jaylin-centered offense. Just like the Bears last week, the Bulldogs were using a "shadow" to stick with Jaylin wherever he went. In fact, they seemed to have figured out that Jaylin couldn't go to his left side. The shadow overplayed Jaylin's right side to force him to his weaker hand.

After five minutes, the score was still tied. DeAndre caught an outlet pass from Mateo, and took off running to midfield.

Jaylin trotted toward the center of the field and prepared to take the pass. Since the Bulldog shadow was on his right, Dee sent a looping pass to Jaylin's left. He and his shadow jostled for position. Jaylin's heart skipped a beat as he felt the ball bounce against the side of his stick and roll off into the center of the field.

A Bulldog middie scooped up the ball and passed it quickly to an attackman running in front of Jaylin and DeAndre. The big attackman caught the ball and ran around behind the goal. He reared back for what looked like a pass to the other side of the field. Suddenly, he fooled the Tigers' defense by executing a slick face dodge and charging straight to the front of the crease. He slipped it under Mateo's stick and into the goal. Bulldogs 5, Tigers 4.

Jaylin growled. This relentless Bulldog defender was getting on his nerves. But maybe he could use it to his team's advantage. After face-off, Jay passed the ball to Damien to start the attack.

"Go forward, Damien," said Jaylin. "Me and my friend will stay back here." He could see his shadow wanted to run back to help on defense, but the guy stayed put. The Tigers sent the ball around the goal a few times, then Greg pulled one of his patented roll dodges and bolted toward the goal. He took a shot, but it bounced off the goal and into the middle where Zach was waiting. Zach swatted the ball quickly into the net hockey-style.

Tie game, 5–5.

"Two minutes!" Coach shouted.

Jaylin won the face-off and passed it off to Damien, who pushed the attack forward as Jaylin stayed on the defensive side of midfield again. He didn't want to make another critical mistake by missing a pass this late in the game.

"Jay, you gotta go up," said a voice in his ear.

"They got it covered," Jaylin said.

"No, they don't," DeAndre said as Greg looked around frantically for someone in the middle to pass it to. Jaylin felt a hard push in the back. "Go!"

"You better hold the defense together!" Jaylin said as he ran forward to join the offense.

"I got this. Now you go get that!" DeAndre replied.

"Somebody get something! One minute!" Coach shouted.

The ball went back around the goal to Jaylin's right. Greg ran behind the goal and passed it to Zach on the top left.

Suddenly, Jaylin sprinted straight at the goal. He brushed shoulders with the Bulldogs' center midfielder as he sped by. The ploy worked, causing his shadow to lose a step as he fought to get around his teammate. As Jaylin entered the attack area, Zach whipped the ball into the middle — to Jaylin's left side. He gulped.

It was happening too fast. He couldn't use his feet to put the ball on his right side. His shadow was half a step behind on his right. He tried to imagine where the ball should be and whipped his stick up to the left.

FWIP! He felt the ball land solidly in the mesh of his stick. He cradled it back and forth as his shadow checked his stick in an attempt to dislodge the ball.

Jaylin could hear Coach yelling something from the sideline, but the words didn't register. The world had narrowed down to him and his defender, who was now between him and the goal.

Turning his head to the left, he threw his shoulders and left knee forward. The shadow lunged in that direction. Jaylin quickly shifted his weight onto his right foot and dodged around the shadow and into the center of the attack area. The middle defenseman was waiting for him, using his feet to keep Jaylin from coming any closer.

Without thinking, Jaylin dove to his right and reached his stick back behind his head. Just before he hit the ground, he let loose a laser toward the top left corner of the net. The Bulldog goalie lunged to his right. Too late! The ball whizzed by him into the net.

Tweet! Tweet! Tweet! The Tigers had done it — they had won 6 to 5! They were going to the playoffs!

Jaylin heard shouts. He heard screams. He even heard curses. Then he felt someone land on top of him. It was Zach. Then Greg. Then the whole team piled on top of him.

As he laughed and struggled to breathe under the mass of bodies, he heard Coach shouting from the sidelines. "Don't break his goggles! We need those for the playoffs!"

AUTHOR BIO

Randall Bonser lives with his wife and two teenage kids in Atlanta, Georgia. He has written several books for adults but enjoys writing for children and teens even more. Randall plays and coaches soccer when he's not writing or cooking something delicious in a slow cooker. His office/library is a complete mess, but he knows exactly where everything is.

ILLUSTRATOR BIO

Aburtov has worked as a colorist for Marvel, DC, IDW, and Dark Horse and as an illustrator for Stone Arch Books. He lives in Monterrey, Mexico, with his lovely wife, Alba, and his crazy children, Ilka, Mila, and Aleph.

GLOSSARY

aggressive (uh-GREH-siv)—strong and forceful

converge (Kuhn-VERJ)—to come together and form a single unit

cradle (KRAY-duhl)—to maintain possession of the ball in the pocket of the stick by moving it from side to side in a smooth motion

crease (KREES)—the circular area around the goal in lacrosse

deficit (DEF-uh-sit)—a lessening in amount

face-off (FAYSS-AWF)—when a player from each team battles for possession of the ball to start or restart a play

lunge (LUHNJ)—to move forward quickly and suddenly

scrimmage (SKRIM-ij)—a practice game

shadow (SHAD-oh)—to secretly follow someone closely and watch the person carefully

specialist (SPESH-uh-list)—a person who is an expert at one particular position or play in a game

DISCUSSION QUESTIONS

1. Why does the coach decide to keep Jaylin on defense at the end of chapter 1? Discuss whether you agree or disagree with this decision, and explain why.

2. After Jaylin gets his new glasses and still has trouble catching passes during a game, he asks the coach to move him back to defense. Does he ask for the position change to benefit himself or the team? Explain your answer.

3. At the end of the story, Jaylin makes a catch on his left and scores the game-winning goal. What helps him succeed this time when he had failed at similar plays in the past? Discuss your answers and other ways he could have reacted.

WRITING PROMPTS

1. Jaylin and DeAndre spend extra time practicing Jaylin's catching skills. Write about a time when you spent extra time practicing a skill for a sport. How did the extra practice pay off in a game?

2. When Jaylin moved from defense to midfielder, his team's defense struggled. Write about a time when you changed roles on a team. Describe how the change impacted the performance of the team.

3. Jaylin convinces his mom to buy him goggles by saying they will fit better under his facemask and they won't break as easily as glasses. Write about a time you asked someone to buy you a more, rather than less, expensive item. List the reasons you gave to convince him or her to buy it.

MORE ABOUT LACROSSE FIELDS

A lacrosse field is divided into six key areas:

1. **Attack/Defensive Areas** — the areas on the ends of the field where offensive players try to score goals and defensive players try to prevent goals

2. **Goal** — a 6-foot (1.8-meters) square opening enclosed by a net

3. **Crease** — the circular area around the goal; offensive players are not allowed to enter the crease

4. **Midfield line** — the line in the center of the field separating the offensive and defensive ends; face-offs occur in the center of the midfield line

5. **Wing Area** — the areas were two of the three midfielders must stand until a face-off starts

6. **Penalty box** — the area where players go to wait out their penalties

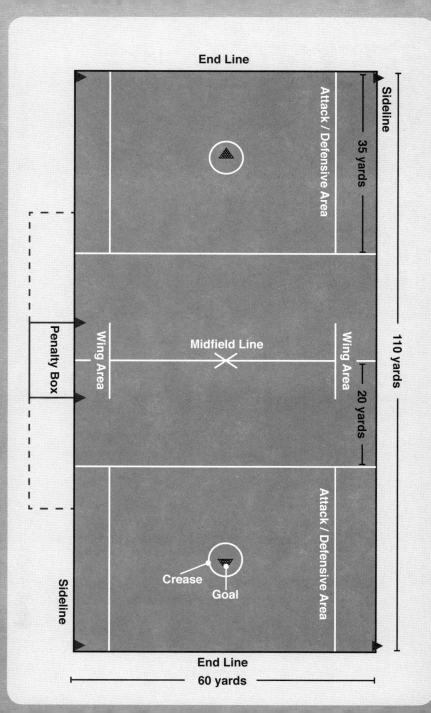

End Line

Sideline

Attack / Defensive Area

35 yards

Penalty Box

Wing Area

Midfield Line

Wing Area

20 yards

110 yards

Sideline

Attack / Defensive Area

Crease

Goal

End Line

60 yards

THE FUN DOESN'T STOP HERE!

DISCOVER MORE AT:

capstonekids.com

Authors and Illustrators
Videos and Contests
Games and Puzzles
Heroes and Villains

Find cool websites
and more books like this one
at www.facthound.com.

Just type in the Book ID:
9781496530516
and you're ready to go!